糖貓
Candy Cat

圖/文　劉品庠

中英
對照

品庠的作品充滿了對動物的愛和單純的真心，
很人溫暖感動！　　　　　富邦基金會董事　陳藹玲

溫暖柔和如棉花糖的筆觸，幾許甜蜜和天真
讓看無窮的想像。　　　　果陀劇場藝術總監　梁志民

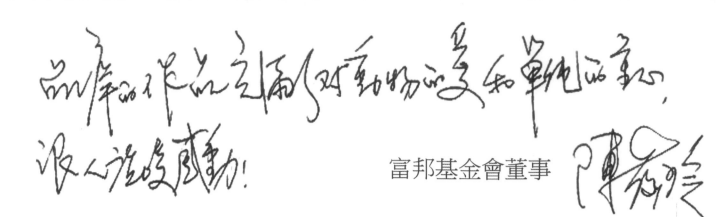

可愛細膩的畫作中，引喻著生命的呵護與共存。
繪本透露出樂觀陽光的日常，
如同菜根譚所云「人心不可一日無喜神」。
品庠擁有柔軟的暖心以及無限的創意，期待未來的創作能更上一層樓，
且佳品源源不絕

國立臺灣藝術大學　設計學院工藝設計學系　系所主任　劉立偉

劉永庠

平常喜歡用相機捕捉貓的身影

發現每一隻貓都有自己的靈性與個性

也應該有牠們自己的故事

如果貓的想法和人的想法碰撞

將會有好多溫暖又有趣的故事發生

YYLTH

傍晚的時候，天空滿滿都是雲，

有一朵雲的形狀好像一隻可愛的小貓。

空氣裡傳來喵…喵…嗚…嗚…的聲音，聽起來好可憐。

天空接著下起雨來，會不會是小貓的眼淚？

It was dusk. The sky was full of clouds.

One cloud stood out because it looked just like the shape of a cute kitten.

The sounds of meow…meow… lingered in air, begging for help.

Then came the rain, as if the kitten were crying.

小女孩琦琦撐起雨傘，看到有一隻流浪貓

躲在路邊的紙箱裡，淋得全身濕透，

冷得一直發抖，發出喵⋯⋯嗚⋯⋯的聲音，

琦琦剛才還以為是那一朵雲在哭，真是好笑。

琦琦看著流浪貓，流浪貓也看著琦琦，

這時候，他們都覺得找到了好朋友。

A little girl named Chichi held up her umbrella and saw a stray cat hiding

in a cardboard box on the side of the road.

Soaked and shivering in the cold, the cat meowed.

It was funny that ChiChi had just thought it was a cloud crying.

ChiChi looked at the stray cat and it looked up at ChiChi. In that magical moment,

they both felt they had found a friend.

琦琦把貓咪抱回家，牠第一個就衝向冰箱，

掛在上面不肯下來，

應該是餓肚子餓了很久了。

ChiChi brought the cat home and it immediately dashed to the top of the refrigerator.

The long-starved cat remained up there, refusing to come down.

貓咪竟然把糖果吃個精光！貓咪還沒有名字，

琦琦發現牠是一隻很愛吃糖果的貓，

所以把牠取名為「**糖貓**」。

The cat ate up all the candy!

The cat did not have a name.

When ChiChi found out that it loved candy,

ChiChi named it **Candy Cat**.

今天是媽媽生日，爸爸特地買了一個大蛋糕。

Today is Mom's birthday and Dad has bought a large cake to celebrate.

來切蛋糕囉！

唉呀！整個蛋糕都已經被糖貓吃光光了！

"Come, everyone! Let's cut the cake."

Oh no! Candy Cat has eaten the entire cake!

糖貓破壞了媽媽的生日，而且牠吃太多東西了。

爸爸決定把牠趕出家門！

琦琦跟在後面，想到要跟糖貓分開，

她很難過，決定偷偷把糖貓帶回家。

Candy Cat had ruined Mom's birthday and Candy Cat had eaten way too much. Dad decided it was time for the cat to leave.

Heart broken, Chichi followed Dad and Candy Cat, deciding to secretly bring the cat back home.

琦琦小心地把糖貓帶回家裡，
把牠藏在房間，不被爸爸發現。

Chichi carefully brought Candy Cat back home

and hid it in her room so that her father would not find out.

琦琦的食量忽然變大，每天都向爸爸要好多東西吃，

爸爸很高興地稱讚琦琦不挑食，一定會長得很高！

爸爸卻不知道那些都是給糖貓吃的。

Chichi's appetite suddenly increased,

everyday she would ask her Dad for more food.

Dad was happy to see ChiChi was no longer being picky, and he believed

Chichi would grow very tall.

He had no idea that all the food was going to Candy Cat.

糖貓吃得實在太多，又關在房間沒有運動，

才短短一個星期，牠就變成一隻大肥貓，

體型是之前的好幾倍！

Candy Cat was eating way too much.

What made it worse was that the cat was stuck in

ChiChi's room without room to move around.

It took only one week for Candy Cat to grow into a big fat cat.

It was several times bigger than before.

為了幫糖貓減肥，琦琦帶著牠在走廊上散步，
而且還要牽著牠，免得牠撞壞家具。

To help Candy Cat lose weight,

ChiChi walked Candy Cat in the house.

During the walk, ChiChi kept Candy Cat on a leash

to keep it from damaging the furniture.

糖貓卻突然往前衝！

琦琦的手沒抓住繩子，她趕緊追了過去……

Suddenly Candy Cat charged forward!

ChiChi was not holding onto the leash,

so all she could do was to chase after Candy Cat.

奶奶沒走好，整個人從樓梯上摔了下來，眼看就要受傷。

忽然，奶奶跌在一坨軟綿綿的東西上面，

感覺很舒服，一點事都沒有。

Elsewhere in the house,

Grandma was trying to walk down the stairs and slipped.

As she fell to the floor, it was clear that she was about to be injured.

But strangely, she landed on something soft and comfortable.

She was completely fine.

奶奶一看，原來是糖貓，是糖貓救了她！

Grandma opened her eyes and realized Candy Cat had saved her.

奶奶把這件事告訴爸爸，爸爸決定原諒糖貓，

並且送牠一個「糖果拉霸機」。

不過，吃糖果要有節制，不然會有蛀牙。

Grandma told Dad about what had happened

and he decided to forgive Candy Cat.

Candy Cat was allowed to stay. Even better, Dad bought

Candy Cat a candy slot machine.

But there was a new house rule. Candy Cat must exercise

self-restraint in eating candy to avoid cavities.

糖貓每個月都要看牙醫，檢查蛀牙。

糖貓每次看牙的時候都大呼小叫，叫到左鄰右舍都聽到。

糖貓流浪的時候認識的好朋友們，他們都擠在窗戶外面看，

一方面笑牠，一方面也羨慕牠，

現在有小主人照顧，每天有東西吃，又不用擔心蛀牙的問題。

Candy Cat had to see the dentist every month, to check for cavities. During each check-up, Candy Cat screamed so loud that the whole neighborhood could hear.

Candy Cat's old friends gathered outside the dentist's office and

watched at Candy Cat from the window.

They laughed at Candy Cat. But they also envied Candy Cat,

because now Candy Cat had a little owner to take care of it.

Candy Cat could have food every day without worrying about cavities.

琦琦他們拍了一張全家福，為了把糖貓拍進畫框，

只好把相機擺得好遠好遠，

人臉都看不清楚，整個畫面都被胖胖的糖貓占滿了。

ChiChi and her family wanted to take a family photo.

But in order to include Candy Cat, they had to position the camera as far as possible.

The faces of ChiChi and her family became completely obscure,

leaving only chubby Candy Cat in focus.

時報悅讀 37

糖貓

作　　　者—劉品孛
封面繪圖—劉品孛
譯　　　者—劉至柔
責任編輯—廖宜家
副 主 編—謝翠鈺
美術編輯—藍天圖物宣字社
封面美編— WST
董 事 長—趙政岷
出 版 者—時報文化出版企業股份有限公司
　　　　　108019 台北市和平西路三段二四〇號七樓
　　　　　發行專線—（〇二）二三〇六六八四二
　　　　　讀者服務專線—〇八〇〇二三一七〇五
　　　　　（〇二）二三〇四七一〇三
　　　　　讀者服務傳真—（〇二）二三〇四六八五八
　　　　　郵撥——一九三四四七二四時報文化出版公司
　　　　　信箱——〇八九九　台北華江橋郵局第九九信箱
時報悅讀網— http://www.readingtimes.com.tw
法律顧問—理律法律事務所　陳長文律師、李念祖律師
印　　　刷—富盛印刷有限公司
初版一刷 一二〇二一年一月二十九日
定　　　價—新台幣二五〇元
缺頁或破損的書，請寄回更換

時報文化出版公司成立於一九七五年，並於一九九九年股票上櫃公開發行，
於二〇〇八年脫離中時集團非屬旺中，
以「尊重智慧與創意的文化事業」為信念。

糖貓/劉品孛作. -- 初版. -- 臺北市：時報文化出
版企業股份有限公司, 2021.1
　面；　公分. --（時報悅讀；37）
ISBN 978-957-13-8478-8（平裝）

863.599　　　　　　　　　　　109018945

ISBN 978-957-13-8478-8
Printed in Taiwan